LOST IN HOLMES COUNTY

Rachel Yoder-May

Lost In Holmes County

Also by Rachel Yoder-May

Courting the Amish Widow

Naomi's Destiny

The Amish Hostage

Lost in Holmes County

Martha's Dilemma

Mary's Christmas Dream

The Amish Scribe

Collections

Amish Romance: Three Books in One (part 1)

Amish Romance: Three Books in One (part 2)

Lost In Holmes County

CHAPTER ONE

Black night. Freezing cold.

Sarah curled up in the fetal position, hoping to banish the cold that made her limbs numb.

The movement made her moan in pain.

She opened her eyes, and the ground whirled her around with a speed that made her close her eyes firmly again.

Taking a deep breath, she waited until the ground stopped moving before she opened them again.

Why was she so dizzy?

She stretched her hand to touch her head and moaned again. Her head hurt… Why?

She struggled to rise from the cold ground

beneath her. The smell of mold and dust tickled her nostrils. She sneezed.

Woah!

Nausea and dizziness overwhelmed her, and she had to lie back again. At least for a moment.

What happened? Why was she lying here? Where was she anyway?

She touched her head again to check if she was bleeding from a wound and noticed that she was wearing a hat of a kind. Her fingers followed the brim to explore the fabric. Was this a bonnet? Why was she wearing a bonnet?

Curious, she looked down herself to check what else she was wearing and saw a blue dress with an apron that looked like its original color was pale pink, but now it was smeared with mud and dirt.

She moved her legs to see what shoes she was wearing and jerked her head back because of the jolt of pain that went through her body. Had she been injured? Why didn't she remember anything?

Slowly, she moved her legs. There they were. Black shoes without ties.

This was definitely an Amish outfit. Was she Amish? She fisted her hands in frustration, when something scratched her left palm. She lifted it up and opened it. A piece of paper?

Narrowing her eyes that had now adjusted to the dim moonlit night she read the note:

Sarah, come and see me. Paul

Her stomach churned, drops of sweats slit down her face in spite of the cold, and she breathed faster.

Why did this note make her afraid? What ghost of a memory had these words scared up?

A sharp wind blew over her and she shuddered. She had to get away from here.

Sarah raised her head and pushed herself into a sitting position. She sat there, breathing, for a few minutes. Then she pushed herself into a squat.

Finally, she was up and stood there, swaying.

"I have to do it. I can stand. I can stand."

She moved one leg forward, searching for safe ground to stand on. Then the next. And after a few more steps, she saw it.

Dim light streaming through the darkness.

Where did it come from?

Sarah narrowed her eyes and stared through the darkness. There. It had to be a farm lying there, not far from where she was. An Amish farm, judging from what she could make out. There were no electric wires near it. No lights outside. Only the dim light that streamed like a gleam of hope through the window.

Her heart pounded faster. She could find help there. Somehow she knew it. And if she were Amish, it would only be the logical place to seek help.

The light showed that someone was still awake in there. She would go there and knock on the door and ask for help.

On wobbling legs and with jolts of pain blurring her view she approached the farm.

CHAPTER TWO

A tall man in his early thirties with red hair and beard opened the door.

He had kind green eyes, which looked at her with curiosity but without hostility, even though she was a stranger – a dirty stranger – knocking on his door.

Her heart beat faster, but this time it wasn't fear. This strange red-haired man stirred emotions in her that she didn't know she had.

Well, she didn't know much about herself at all right now, but somehow she instinctively knew that this feeling was new to her.

"Yes?"

"I need help." She wrestled her hands. Would he let her in?

"Come in." The man opened the door the rest of the way and showed her in with a gesture of his hand.

She stepped inside and the cramping in her body, caused by the cold, relaxed a bit.

The door clicked shut behind them.

"What happened to you?" The man frowned, and she realized that she must look terrible. If all those places where her head hurt were bruises, she would be covered by a pattern of blue, red and white.

"I don't know."

"Your face is bruised…"

"I don't remember what happened."

"Oh!" He frowned even more. "Let's go to the living room. Then we can talk more about that."

Somehow the little farmhouse looked familiar to her. She had no recollection of seeing it before, but she felt at home.

It was clean, simple and cozy.

One pair of man's shoes was placed on a doormat next to one pair of clean boots. She took off her shoes and placed them next to the boots.

The wooden floor felt warm against her

cold sock-clad feet and she enjoyed the touch of the smooth surface that made no sound when she stepped over it.

The man led her into a larger room with blue curtains and a lamp casting a cozy light over the plain wooden furniture and the upholstered couch along one side of the walls.

There were no paintings on the white walls, and the floor was bare except for two homemade rugs.

"Please sit down. I'll make us a cup of tea."

Sarah looked at the couch. "I'll get it dirty."

He smiled. "Don't worry. The cloth is water repellent. Pure wool. I can easily clean off any dirt tomorrow."

She sat down on the edge of the couch and the man turned away, probably to make the tea he had promised.

Four minutes later he entered the room again. Sarah had closed her eyes to relax and see if any memories arose, when she smelled the pleasant scent of camomile and lemon. She swallowed. Her mouth was dry and she suddenly realized that she was both hungry and thirsty.

"I brought some bread and butter, too. Here." He handed her a steaming cup of tea and a plate with a huge lump of bread, generously buttered. Her mouth watered.

"Thank you. That was kind of you." She took a sip of the tea and then bit into the bread. Mmmm... She closed her eyes. This was so delicious. She opened her eyes again and found his green eyes watching her. Her cheeks felt warm and she curled her toes. Was he waiting for her to say something?

"This is good. Did you – or your wife – bake it yourself?"

"I did. And churned the butter. My wife – sadly – passed away a few years ago."

"Oh, I'm sorry." So why did her heart jump again and beat like crazy?

The man took a sip of his tea and then put down the cup. "I'm such a rude. Please forgive my manners. I haven't even introduced myself. I'm Dannie Troyer." He stretched out his hand to meet hers.

"Sarah ... Sarah."

"Sarah Sarah? That's a very unusual name." There was a glimpse of humor in his eyes. She liked it.

"I don't remember my last name. In fact..." She bit her lower lip. "I don't remember my first name either, but I assume it's Sarah, because I was clutching this when I woke up." She handed him the note.

Dannie studied it and handed it back to her. "Who's Paul?"

She shook her head and shivered.

"He scares you somehow?"

"Yes."

"What do you remember about him?"

"Nothing." She smoothed the piece of paper, but nothing came to mind.

"Could he be your husband or fiancé?"

Wouldn't she remember him if she were in love with him? Maybe. Maybe not. She shrugged. "I don't know. He could be anybody. I don't remember anything about him. Not his looks, not his voice... Nothing. But I... His name scares me. That's all I know."

She thought again about Dannie's question. Could Paul be her fiancé or husband? A quick glance at her hands revealed no rings. So she wasn't engaged or married. Who was this Paul then?

Her heart beat faster and she started to shake. Suddenly she was overwhelmed with fear. She had to get away. But where to?

And how? Her eyes sought the door.

Then Dannie's hand covered hers.

"Don't worry. We'll get to the bottom of this."

She wanted to believe him. But she wasn't so sure.

He squeezed her hands. "Trust me."

Her face reflected in his eyes. She looked pale.

She met his gaze. "I trust you."

CHAPTER THREE

The long winding road was surrounded by grass and flowers and a few trees. Birds were singing and Sarah listened to the clip-clopping of the horse and the wind sliding through the leaves.

Next to her, Dannie was driving the buggy. They had decided to ask for help from the local police, since nobody in the Amish county Dannie lived in had seen Sarah before.

Had she ever been to a police station before? Sarah had no idea. The place didn't seem familiar to her, but faces looked friendly as she and Dannie were led to a police officer.

The police officer was a young man in his thirties. He was tall and skinny, with a black mustache and short, black hair. He invited them to sit down on the office chairs in front of his desk that was neat and only contained a few items: Pencils, pens, paper, and a mug that said "Joe's Cup" on one side and "A Cup of Joe" on the other.

"I'm officer White. What can I do for you?"

Sarah saw him switch his gaze from her to Dannie and back again. Apparently, Amish people didn't seek his help every day.

"We would like to know if you have heard of any missing Amish women."

Joe White widened his eyes. "Missing Amish? Not that I know of, but let me check."

He leaned to the left and turned on the computer that stood on a small table next to his desk. It buzzed and came to life. He hummed a little tune but didn't touch the keyboard before the computer was ready. Then he typed in a few instructions. The computer dinged and he studied the screen. He turned towards them.

"No, I'm sorry. No missing Amish women. No missing Amish at all, in fact."

"No?" Dannie pursed his lips and tapped his fingertips against them.

Sarah looked down on her hands. They were shaking. Could it be that no one was missing her? Or didn't her community think they should alert the authorities yet?

She fisted her fingers to stop her hands from shaking, cleared her throat and addressed the officer. "Maybe the information hasn't arrived on your computer yet?" She hoped this was the case.

"No, miss. With this technology, the news arrives instantly. The moment I add a file to the computer, they can find it in all the neighboring police areas. I'm sorry."

She sighed. This was peculiar. She had to be missing, since she was here, alone, away from home.

Dannie seemed to sense her disappointment. He grabbed her hand and held it under the table. Then he leaned forward with a smile.

"What if Sarah came from a community that's outside of your jurisdiction? Would that show up in your computer?"

Joe White studied the computer screen for a moment. Then he frowned. "If Miss Sarah went missing in another precinct, then we wouldn't be able to see a missing person report until the following day. But you've been here since yesterday, right?" He turned towards Sarah, who nodded.

He pinched his lips. "Then we should have received the missing persons report by now. It could happen, though. If your community either didn't know you had disappeared or for some reason decided to wait rather than contact their local police …" His voice trailed away.

"But we won't know until tomorrow?" Sarah squeezed Dannie's hand. There was hope. All wasn't lost.

"I can ask around, but no, we probably won't know anything until tomorrow."

"I can live with that." She let go of Dannie's hand and pushed back her chair. Dannie also stood up.

"Thank you, officer. You've been most helpful."

Joe White got up and shook Dannie's hand. "You're welcome."

Sarah curtsied and turned around to leave with Dannie. They didn't know more than when they arrived, but she had a frail hope now. By this time tomorrow, she might know who she was and what she was doing

Lost In Holmes County

here.

CHAPTER FOUR

The horse and buggy were waiting outside the police station where they'd left it. Dannie clapped the muzzle of the dark brown gelding and was greeted with a welcoming snort.

Obviously there was a bond between this man and his horse. Sarah smiled. Then she went over to the side of the buggy. Dannie opened the door for her and took her arm, but she jumped right up.

He laughed. "You've obviously done this before. It's as if you've done nothing else since you were a little girl."

She giggled. "Yes, I guess I must have taken a lot of buggy rides. Maybe I have my own buggy?"

"You probably have." A cloud passed in front of the sun and cast a shadow on his face. "Unless your fiancé drove you around in his buggy."

"I don't think so. I mean... I don't remember, of course, but wouldn't I remember if I was engaged?"

He nodded slowly. "Probably, yes."

Did his eyes light up? She watched him go to the other side of the buggy.

With an agile jump he got up and sat next to her, shook the reins and smiled. "I have an idea."

"You do?"

"Clearly your body remembered getting up a buggy. Maybe your body remembers other things? Like freezing, sweating, being happy... What if I ask you some questions and we'll see how you react?"

"Anything that might help. Go ahead."

"Okay..." He bit his lips then turned towards her. "I will study your every reaction, so you might find this creepy. I'm only doing this to help."

"Sure." She patted his hand. "I know you are."

"Good. Here we go. First word:

Christmas."

She shrugged and shook her head.
"Nothing."

"Easter?"

"No."

"Summer."

She shook her head.

"Church."

She looked at him and pursed her lips.

"Singing."

She sighed.

"Barn raising."

"Grass. I remember the smell of grass. And freshly dug soil."

"Great, that's a start. It doesn't tell us where you come from, but a start."

"Yes." Her heart beat faster now. There was hope. Her body remembered. What more would he be able to uncover?

"Wedding."

She was aware that her gaze flickered. What did "wedding" remind her body of? She didn't know, but she felt uncomfortable.

"Paul."

Sarah jumped in her seat. Her heart beat so hard now that she could hear it. "Paul" scared her. But why? What had he tried to do? Who was he?

"So you remember Paul."

"Kind of. I don't know who he is, but the sound of his name scares me."

Dannie didn't answer.

He turned towards the road ahead of him, and for several minutes they sat in silence. The only sounds heard were the wind rustling the leaves and the horse's clip-clopping on the road. A bird sang somewhere over the field and a bee buzzed by. Otherwise there was silence.

She started to relax again. It felt so good to sit here next to Dannie. It was as if she'd known him all her life. She felt safe. And happy.

Dannie was still looking straight ahead when he talked again. "This might not work…"

"You have another idea?"

He nodded. "Yes, but I'm not sure how to do it right. It's something I heard about a long time ago. How sounds and rhythms can … kind of make you relaxed. Lull you almost into sleep. And in that state your mind remembers things your brain has forgotten."

"Oh, I know what that is. Hypnosis, right?"

He nodded. "I just don't know how to use it, so this idea might not work at all." He was still staring straight ahead, as if he was afraid to ask her directly and see her reaction.

"I trust you. Let's try your idea." She leaned back against the seat. "Go ahead. I'm all yours."

Dannie cleared his throat. "Okay, then… if you want. Then close your eyes."

She did as told.

"Listen to the horse's clip-clopping. Focus on that sound. This is all you can hear."

He stayed quiet for a while and she listened to the sound of the horse's hooves hitting the hard road.

Then he spoke again. "What do you remember? When have you heard that sound before?"

She didn't know. She didn't remember ever having heard it before until today, but she must have. She knew how to jump up and place herself on the seat next to the driver, and it was very unlikely that she - as an Amish person - should never have driven in a buggy before.

Sarah squeezed her eyes hard in an effort to remember, but nothing came up.

Dannie continued. "Imagine that I'm driving you home. What do you see? What do you smell? Where does the road lead us?"

She shook her head and opened her eyes.

Nothing had come to mind. Nothing at all. This was hopeless.

CHAPTER FIVE

Yellow sunbeams streamed in through the high barn windows and made dust from the hay shine like a thousand golden sparkles.

Sarah giggled as the brown calf pushed its muzzle against her hand. She petted the animal on top of its head and the calf moved closer to her, sticking its big head down the bucket she held in her right hand.

"No, no, you can go to your mother. She'll feed you. This is for the goats." She moved the bucket outside the calf's field of vision, and it turned around. She saw it push its muzzle against the big brown cow, who just kept chewing its hay.

Dannie approached her with a grin. His

freckles seemed to glow in the afternoon sun that lit up his red hair and made it look like a glowing halo around his kind face. Her heart beat faster.

"I see that you met Mandy."

"Is that the calf's name?"

When Dannie nodded, she continued, "You name all your animals?"

"Yeah, that makes it easier to call them when it's feeding time. Wanna see?"

She couldn't wait.

"Okay, let's go to the hencoop. I was just about to feed them anyway. We can see to your goats afterwards. There aren't as many of them."

Sarah followed him, enjoying the little tune he was humming. He walked across the court yard to a small area surrounded by chicken wire, with wooden door. There was a small henhouse inside where the chicken would spend the night and rainy days, but right now they were all picking the ground outside.

The door opened without a sound in spite of its old hinges.

"Ready?" Dannie lifted his bucket a few inches and thrust his hand into the mix of grains and green leaves it contained.

She nodded so hard that her kapp almost fell off. This was exciting.

"Chook, chook," Dannie said and two hens ran towards him. "Chook, chook, chook, chook," he continued and more chickens approached him.

"You're not calling them by their names," Sarah said.

"Oh, yes, I am. This is Chook, and this is Chook. Oh, and meet Chook and Chook."

She giggled. "What about the brown chicken over there? Why didn't she come? What's her name?"

"That's Clarice. She never comes when I call Chook, Chook or Chook. Only when I call her name." He dipped his hand in the bucket and grabbed a handful of chicken food. "Clarice, come," he said with a loud and clear voice. And the brown chicken ran to him.

"She knows her name? Like a dog?"

"Of course, why wouldn't she?"

Sarah was stunned and she was just about to ask Dannie how he'd trained his chickens to do this when the sound of tires and a running engine announced the arrival of a car in the courtyard.

Dannie raised an eyebrow and they both

left the hencoop to greet the stranger.

The car was a black and white Ford with the word Police written on its sides. The driver opened the door and stepped out. He was tall, slender and muscular, wearing a cap and sunglasses.

"Dannie Troyer?"

"That's me."

"Ma'am." The policeman tipped his cap in the direction of Sarah.

"What can we do for you?" Dannie stretched out his hand to greet the officer. He was taller than the policeman and just as muscular. Working on a farm made it unnecessary to go to a gym.

"Officer White sent me, I'm Officer Andrews. He's been in phone contact with the authorities in all jurisdictions adjacent to Amish areas. Nobody has contacted them about missing persons matching your description. I'm sorry, ma'am."

Nobody missed her? That couldn't be true. Why had nobody reported her missing?

Dannie put his arm around her shoulder and it comforted her a little.

"Thank you for letting me know, Officer."

"You're welcome." The policeman turned

around and opened the door to his car, when his radio crackled. He sat down on the driver seat and grabbed the microphone. "Yes?"

"Officer Andrews, we had an assault attempt with a deadly weapon in your neighborhood. We'll send back-up, but look out for a 30-year-old caucasian male. He's violent and dangerous."

Sarah took four steps backwards. Her legs swayed. Her stomach churned and she felt the blood rush from her head. She had to sit down now. As if coming from far away, she heard Officer Andrews reply.

"Understood. What more can you tell me about him? Clothes? Looks? Name?"

The radio crackled again and Sarah only caught two words: Code 245.

Through a mist she saw Officer Andrews put the microphone back and get out of the car again. He spoke to Dannie. "There's a dangerous man in the neighborhood. He probably won't come here, but if you notice any strangers, don't approach them. Just call us."

"I don't have a phone."

"Oh... Yes, of course." The officer tapped his belt. "Is there any way you can warn us if you see somebody sneaking around here?"

"I don't know. Probably not. Unless if I can sneak out and grab the buggy and drive to town."

"Let's hope he doesn't show up." The policeman got inside his car again.

Sarah cleared her throat. "What... is his... name?"

She already knew the answer. It had to be Paul. Only that would explain why she got so scared when she heard about the violent man. She must have fled him and now he was following her. There was no other explanation.

"His name? Does his description remind you of somebody?" He looked at her over the top of the window.

She nodded. "Maybe. I'm not sure. Is his name Paul?"

"No. His name is Michael. Good day to you." He closed the door and started the engine.

Sarah stood motionless and followed his car with her eyes as he left the farm.

CHAPTER SIX

Two hours later, Sarah still felt shaken by the news about the violent man. His name wasn't Paul, but the policeman's words kept sounding in her head. "Assault attempt with a deadly weapon."

Was it this man she was afraid of? Or did it have nothing to do with him? She'd just been in a violent situation that had scared her. Maybe she was traveling on her own in a buggy and the horse had run wild.

No, that couldn't be it, because somebody would have found the runaway horse by now and reported it. Everybody recognized an Amish buggy, so the police would have heard about it if that was what had happened.

Could she have fallen and hit her head and just imagined this fear that the name Paul induced in her?

Sarah didn't know, but she was going crazy thinking about this. She had to do something physical to clear her mind. She'd felt so good feeding the animals this afternoon with Dannie.

Her heart beat faster every time she thought of him, who'd taken in a stranger in his house and treated her like a long-time friend.

The thought made her a little sad. She wasn't sure she was satisfied by being just a friend. She was attracted to Dannie. His happy green eyes, his lively freckles, his burning red hair and beard, his tall, muscular frame... All of him made her long to be with him everyday, working together, chatting, laughing, talking.

She loved being with him, and she wanted it to never end.

Right now he was humming in the kitchen, preparing dinner. He'd asked her to sit here and relax, but it drove her mad. Why not go and ask if she could help with something?

Sarah got up and walked to the kitchen.

The room was big and welcoming. The kitchen was situated at the corner of the house with several big windows on the northern wall, and a door and another big window to the east. The sun had sunk down into its deep red sea behind the hills a short while ago, so Dannie had lit gas lights that cast a warm glow over the interior of the room.

He turned around from the iron cast stove by the eastern wall when she entered. Seeing his big smile made her heart go bouncing up and down.

"Can I help you with something, Dannie?"

"I thought you were relaxing? You've been through a lot, and I'm sure you need it."

"I need to do something or the thoughts and questions will drive me crazy. All this is a mystery. My brains keep churning around, leaving me no peace."

"Alright, then, why don't you give me a hand with the bread? I've made the dough and it's rising at the moment. It should be ready in fifteen minutes, so if you would heat the kochoffe while I peel the potatoes, that would help me."

"Good, I'll do that."

Dannie stepped aside and went to a pantry where he grabbed a small sack of potatoes. He picked ten big ones and put the sack back. "Don't worry, you don't have to eat them all at once. I always cook for several days. Makes it easier just to heat the food the following day, doesn't it?"

"It certainly does."

Right, she had to start heating the oven. She looked at the stove. Where should she start? She placed her hand on the iron plate that covered the whole stove top. It was cold. There were circular rings on its surface, obviously meant to place pots and pans on. It had four short legs, and when she squatted in front of it, looking for the oven, she saw two doors with wide handles.

She dragged one of the handles and peeked inside a clean oven. There was a slight scent of bread and cookies inside. But where did she light it? Obviously, there was no electrical switch on it.

She used the handle to the left and opened up a smaller compartment that smelled of wood and fire. The walls had small traces of soot on them, although it definitely had been cleaned after the last use.

Sarah blinked back tears of disappointment. She wanted to help, but this memory loss of hers went deeper than she thought. She didn't even remember how to heat the oven. And she couldn't figure it out just by looking at it.

She cleared her throat. "I don't remember how to do it."

Dannie rinsed a potato and dropped it in a huge pot. "That's okay. I'm done with the potatoes now, so I can do it."

"Will you show me how you start the oven? Then maybe I will remember…"

"Of course." He dried his hands in a towel and approached her. "Here's the wood." He pointed to a basket on the floor behind the stove. She hadn't noticed it sitting there. "You take two or three pieces of wood, depending on the baking time, and put it inside the compartment to the left. The one you just opened."

Sarah opened it again and inserted three pieces of chopped wood.

"Good. Then you take one of these tablets…" He grabbed a kindling tablet from a box inside the same basket, "… put it on top of the wood. You take a match stick and then you light the tablet."

She did as told, but it stirred no memories inside her. This could just as well have been the first time she heated an oven as the thousandth time.

"Well done. It's funny that you remembered the name, kochoffe, but not how to light it."

"Yes. I wonder why."

"It will all come back to you, I'm sure."

Sarah forced herself to smile. Hopefully it would. But when?

Dannie took the pot of potatoes and water and placed it on top of the kitchen stove. There was a sizzling sound coming from the top as a few remaining drops of water evaporated from the bottom.

"The oven will be warm soon, so I'll shape the dough while it's heating."

Fifty minutes later they sat down to eat. The dinner Dannie had prepared was simple but smelled delicious. Sarah's stomach roared in anticipation as she sat down in front of Dannie and unfolded the napkin and placed it in her lap.

He smiled at her, and her heart jumped when she saw the warm glow in his green eyes.

She felt happy right now and here.

With his eyes still fixed on her, Dannie folded his hands and said, "Let's pray."

Sarah felt the blood leave her head. She froze. Pray?

She had no idea what to say or what to do. There was no recollection at all. Not even the faintest idea.

Maybe if I start by doing whatever Dannie does? Sarah folded her hands, closed her eyes and bowed her head.

Nothing came to her.

Her heart beat so fast and loud now that she was sure Dannie would hear it. She opened one eye a little bit and looked at him. He seemed deep in prayer.

What should she do?

She closed her eyes again, hoping for a miracle. Weren't prayers supposed to give rise to miracles?

After a deep breath, she felt slightly more relaxed, but no words of prayer came to her.

Then she heard Dannie take a deep breath too. She looked up, and he was smiling at her.

"I'm glad to see that there's something you do remember," he said and patted her hands.

Her throat was dry and it was as if she'd been walking in the desert for hours.

Slowly she shook her head.

"What's wrong?" His smile disappeared and he looked worried.

"I didn't remember. I... I... don't know how to pray. I tried to, but..."

Dannie's hand was still resting on hers and now he grabbed them with his other hand too and folded them. He gave her folded hands a squeeze.

"It will come back to you. Don't worry. This is how you should do it."

She leaned forward towards him. She wanted to be sure to get everything right so she put her full attention on what he was about to say.

"First you fold your hands. You already did so earlier, which is why I thought you remembered. Then you close your eyes and bow your head. Then you say this prayer silently. I'll say it out loud now, but you're supposed to say the prayer in your head. Got it?"

"Yes."

"Here we go."

He folded his own hands, closed his eyes and bowed his head. Sarah followed his lead.

O Lord God, heavenly Father, bless us and these thy gifts, which we shall accept from thy tender goodness.

Give us food and drink also for our souls unto life eternal, and make us partakers of thy heavenly table through Jesus Christ. Amen.

Our Father, which art in heaven, hallowed be thy name;

thy kingdom come; thy will be done, in earth as it is in heaven.

Give us this day our daily bread.

And forgive us our trespasses, as we forgive them that trespass against us.

And lead us not into temptation; but deliver us from evil.

For thine is the kingdom, the power, and the glory, for ever and ever.

Amen.

When Dannie stopped praying, she felt good. She couldn't remember ever having heard the prayer before, but it worked.

She felt peace, trust and love.

Sarah opened her eyes and her gaze met Dannie's.

Trust and love.

CHAPTER SEVEN

Sarah was doing the dishes and enjoying the sun through the kitchen window when Dannie came rushing in through the door.

He looked disturbed.

His normally well-ordered red hair stuck out in all directions, and his red freckles stood out against his pale skin. He slammed the door shut behind him and turned the key around in its lock.

"What's wrong?" She had no doubt that something terrible must have happened. He was normally so calm.

"The manager of the grocery store, Anthony, he got a black eye."

"Oh, that was terrible. What happened to

him?"

"The black eye isn't the worst. It's what he told me that's really bad."

"What did he say?"

"When I asked him who gave him his bruises, he said that it was a stranger."

"A stranger? Like a tourist coming to see Holmes County?"

He narrowed his lips and shook his head. "Didn't sound like it. This guy came into his store and asked him if there was an Englisch woman living here."

"Strange question."

"It gets even more strange. When Anthony said 'no', the stranger beat him up."

"Why would he do that?" Sarah dried her hands in the kitchen towel.

"Don't know. Maybe he didn't believe him? Or maybe he was frustrated? Anyway, he became violent and punched him in his face."

Sarah suddenly felt dizzy. Her legs went weak under her, and she reached out to grab one of the wooden kitchen chairs to sit down.

"Sarah, what's happening? Did this remind you of something? You're so pale."

He went to the cupboard and grabbed a clean glass, filled it with fresh water from the gas-driven refrigerator and gave it to her. "Here, drink. It will help you."

She took the glass and drank for a while, until she felt slightly better. "Thanks," she said and put down the glass.

"What happened there?"

"I don't know. I... the violence. Dannie, I'm scared. And I don't know why. I wish I could remember everything. This is so frustrating. I'm afraid and I don't know what to do about it to be safe."

He seized her shoulders, squatted down in front of her and hugged her against his strong chest. "You're safe here. If a stranger comes here, all of the Gmay will protect you."

"Your community is so nice. You must love it here."

"Been here all my life, but yes, I love it. Like you must have loved your community."

If only she remembered. And why hadn't they reported her missing? That thought puzzled her again.

Would her community have helped her?

Dannie released her and got up again.

"Don't worry." He smiled at her. "Like I said, you're safe here among the Amish."

His words were meant to make her calm, but they had the opposite effect. Her heart was racing like a horse towards the finish line and blood rushed from her face.

"Safe here among the Amish." His words echoed through her head and stirred up the shade of a memory.

No, she wasn't safe here. She knew it with a strange certainty.

Could this Paul of hers be Amish and violent?

She closed her eyes to call up more memories, but nothing came to her.

Dannie squatted in front of her again, looked her in her eyes and said, "You don't feel safe here, do you?"

His lovely face looked so serious and sad. She hated to hurt him.

With a sigh she confessed. No, she didn't feel safe here. Not even in Dannie's home.

CHAPTER EIGHT

Dannie dragged out a chair and sat down next to her. It was past noon now, and they should have been preparing lunch, but too much had happened.

"What do you remember?"

"I don't know. When you told me of this violent man, it reminded me of something." She sighed. "But that's it. I don't remember faces or names or situations or anything."

"It's a start, though. But think about it. Why did it affect you to hear about a violent man?"

She looked down, trying to focus on the thought. A violent man. What did it remind her of? Had she had an encounter with a violent man? Was that how she got all those bruises? Who was that violent man? Paul? Was he Amish like her? No Amish were violent, were they?

Her stomach churned and she felt nauseous.

She kept hearing those words in her head... "Safe here among the Amish. Safe among the Amish. Not safe among the Amish."

She got up so fast that her chair turned over and landed on the floor with a huge clash. "I'm not safe here."

"Are you sure? Why wouldn't you be safe here? Nobody comes here."

"I don't know why, but I know it now. I'm not safe here. I have to leave."

Dannie looked sad, or was he just worried for her safety?

She grabbed his hands. "I'm sorry, Dannie, but I have to leave. I'm not safe here. I'm not safe anywhere, I think... but here I risk putting you in danger as well. And I don't want that. You've been so helpful. You took me in – a stranger. You accepted me in your house."

Dannie got up too and hugged her against him. She could smell his clean shirt and feel his warmth. If only she could stay here with him. Tears threatened to fall from her eyes and she blinked them back.

"Stay here, Sarah. We'll face the danger together. Together we're stronger."

"No. I can't accept that. You don't know what's waiting out there. Even I don't. I just know that I have to get away. Now. Please, help me to get away from here. I have to leave now."

She was crying now. Not tears of pity, but salty tears of fear. She was terrified that anything might happen to Dannie, who'd become such a dear friend in only a few days.

She felt so close to him.

She wished she could stay forever in this little farmhouse. Helping him feed the animals and name them when they were born. Wash his dishes and bake his bread. Cook his meals and sweep the floor. Even churn homemade butter, once he'd shown her how to do that, because that was another thing she didn't remember.

She wished she could do all that for him. But that would put him in danger, and she wasn't going to allow that to happen.

No, her mind was made up. She had to

leave now and maybe never see Dannie again.

She would be leaving him and his safe home to enter the unknown.

Sarah was ready. She had no choice.

Ready to leave the man she now knew she loved.

CHAPTER NINE

Dannie helped Sarah up. She sat in the buggy, wearing a clean dress, apron and bonnet that had belonged to his late wife. There hadn't been time to wash her only dress, and since she'd arrived without luggage, she didn't have anything clean with her.

The comfortable dress, a little larger than what she was wearing when she arrived, carried a slight scent of lavender, which brought back a fragment of a memory, of an old lady who'd been close to her. Her grandmother? Hopefully it would all come back to her soon. Not knowing her own history was so frustrating.

Dannie jumped up next to her and grabbed the reins. "Where to?"

She shook her head. She had no idea. The only thing she knew was that she had to get out of here. "Take me to the station. Then I'll get on the first train that arrives."

"Okay, then. The station."

He turned his head and raised his arms to shake the reins when a car entered the farmyard with screeching tires.

The driver slammed on the brakes and the car stopped right next to Sarah's side of the buggy.

Her heart was racing, and she didn't move. Let him go away, let him go away.

A short, muscular man rushed out of the car. He had square jaws, dark hair and dark eyes.

Sarah gasped and put both hands in front of her mouth.

The stranger ran towards her and without stopping, he reached out to grab her.

Sarah screamed.

Suddenly she remembered everything.

"Help," she screamed, but the man already had his hands on her, dragging her towards the ground.

She planted her feet against the door step

of the buggy to resist, but he was stronger than her. In a moment, she would be at his mercy. Now she knew why she'd been running away from that man. And it was critical to keep out of his reach.

This was the man she'd fled. This was Michael Simons, her former fiancé.

And he was about to win the fight. His pull was so strong that she felt herself being lifted out of the seat. In a moment he would have her in his power and drag her into his car and drive away with her. And she wasn't certain she would survive that encounter.

Then she felt Dannie's arm around her waist. With his right arm, he dragged her back. Thank God he was so strong.

The moment her body hit the seat again, he shook the reins with his left hand and the buggy jumped forward.

She just had time to see Michael getting knocked over as the buggy sped past.

"Let's get to the police station." Dannie looked over his shoulder back at the man, lying in his courtyard. "Good, he is unconscious. That should give us time."

As if the horse understood the urgency, it ran faster than ever before.

For the first time since she'd decided to leave Dannie, Sarah felt safe.

She turned towards Dannie, the only man she had ever loved. She trusted him.

Her throat was dry and she swallowed. She had trust and love. What about him? Did he feel the same way, or had he only helped her out of pity?

Michael was knocked over, but her problems weren't solved.

She still had a terrible secret and there was no way around it.

Sarah pouted her lips and took a deep breath.

She had to tell Dannie her secret.

CHAPTER TEN

Sarah stood in the farm yard and watched the last of the police cars drive off.

As soon as they'd mentioned the violent man being in Dannie's farmyard, several policemen jumped into their cars to arrest him.

When the dust settled she raised her face and smiled at Dannie, who had his arm around her waist. He smiled back.

"Do you feel safe now?"

"Yes. Now I finally feel safe. Michael is not going to get out of jail anytime soon."

"No, between beating you up, giving the manager a black eye and the incidents of violence on his record, he's going to be put away for a long time."

She nodded. To think that she'd been engaged to that man.

Dannie put his index finger on the tip of her nose. "Why do I get the feeling that something is bothering you?"

Had he sensed that? She looked down.

"Dannie, there's something I have to tell you."

"If you mean you and that violent guy having been engaged, it's okay. I guess he seduced you and you didn't know any better. Of course, you shouldn't have trusted an Englischer." He winked and she got it. He was only half-joking. This joke hurt, though.

"No, that's not it. It's something else."

"Let's go inside. We still haven't had lunch, and I'm starving. I'm sure it's nothing so terrible that we can't talk about it inside."

It was terrible, but it wouldn't make a difference whether she told him her secret out here in the yard or inside his nice, neat home.

The home she'd come to appreciate and love.

He turned her around, and still with his

arm around her back, they walked together towards the house.

"You said you got your memory back, right?"

"Yes." She took off her shoes right inside the door and put them on the mat next to Dannie's boots.

"Good, then you can light the stove top to heat the food I made yesterday. I'll lay the table."

"Dannie, about my memory…"

"Yes? You do remember everything, don't you? You told me that you remembered this guy, Michael, beating you. And you remembered fleeing and getting help from your friend Paul."

"That's not all I remember. You see… Maybe you should sit down first. Then you'll understand."

They sat down around the little kitchen table. Dannie frowned.

"I know I sound weird, but what I have to tell you… It's not easy for me to do."

"I can't imagine anything being that terrible, so go ahead."

"Paul is a friend of mine."

"Yes, you told me so."

"I didn't tell you how I got to know him. I

grew up on a farm near his. We were childhood friends. For a while we even went to the same school."

"Of course, like all Amish children."

"Dannie..." She took a deep breath. "I'm not Amish."

"What?" His eyes were huge and dark green against his pale skin.

If only she could reach out and touch his glowing red hair, but she had to tell him this. She had to know how he would react.

"I'm an atheist. Or rather, I was. I'm not so sure anymore. But I grew up in a non-religious family. I'm an Englischer, Dannie. I'm sorry."

"You're an Englischer? I can't believe it. You seem to fit in so well. You're like a typical Amish. Look at you... Here you are in a blue dress with a kapp and apron."

"I know. Paul gave me his wife's dress to wear so I would look Amish. He tried to hide me from Michael."

"But it didn't work?"

"No. He sent me this note – the note I was clutching when I woke up. He found out that Michael had tracked me down and was on his way to get me. So he arranged for somebody to drive me to another Amish neighborhood, where nobody had heard of me, so that I could be safe from Michael. Your neighborhood."

"Then what happened? Did he get to you and beat you and let you lie there in the dark?"

She shook her head. "No. I got the bruises before Paul helped me and kept me hidden in his home. But when I arrived here in the car, I asked the driver to let me out a little away from the Amish community. I wanted to walk the last stretch myself to get some fresh air and clear my thoughts.

"Unfortunately, I passed out. I must have been overwhelmed and scared, because I was on my own and didn't know what the future would bring. When I woke up, I'd lost my memory. I found your house, and the rest, you know."

"What are your plans now?" His face didn't reveal what he felt. Did he hate her for not being Amish?

"I don't know. Dannie, something happened to me while I was living here with you. I didn't remember any prayers, because I'd never learned any. You taught me how to pray. You stirred something up in my heart. I believe, now. I believe in the Lord and his love. And also..." She looked down her hands. They were shaking.

"Yes?"

"I loved living here like this. The simple life." Her voice was very low, almost a whisper. She was drained. But Dannie had to know it all. Her new faith, her love for him. If only he would give a hint about what he felt.

"Then what's the problem?"

"What?"

"I mean, it seems clear to me. You have found faith. You like the Amish life... Sarah..." He cupped her hands around her chin. "Do you like me just a little bit?"

She swallowed and nodded.

"Then it's clear to me what you should do."

"It is?"

"Yes. Stay here on my farm. I've loved you since the moment I opened the door and saw you standing there. You looked so lost. All beaten up and dirty. And yet, I could tell there was goodness and love in your heart."

He smiled. "Allow me to court you, Sarah. Convert and become Amish, if your heart agrees with it. And then hopefully, over time, you'll come to love me as I love you, and we'll marry and have children."

"Oh, Dannie, you're crazy, and I already love you."

"Then it's settled." He grabbed her hands and looked her in her eyes. "Sarah, may I court you?"

"You may," she said and felt the heat in her cheeks.

He turned her right hand palm-up and gave it a kiss. "Then please heat our food. I'm starving."

She giggled.

The future looked bright.

She had not only found the memory that she'd lost. She'd also found trust, faith and love.

Life was good.

The End

Following is a sample from *Martha's Dilemma*.

Finally.

Martha opened the lid on the wooden chest in the corner of the living room and drew out a box of color pencils. In a few minutes, she would be playing around with all those lovely colors. She smiled. Careful not to shake the box and ruin the fragile pencil leads, she pushed away the table cloth and put the box down.

The room smelled of coffee, home-baked bread and freshly-churned butter from the breakfast she and her family had just enjoyed.

As she hummed a little tune, she took the

easel from behind the door and pushed the legs to each side to stand it up before she placed a big sketching pad on top of it.

Sun streamed in through the square window. Martha squeezed one eye shut as the light hit the white paper and reflected in her face.

Maybe she should draw the view through that window. The way the blue curtains framed the violet and pink flowers outside, it would make a beautiful, romantic picture.

If only I could grab the smell of the violets and roses too.

Still humming, she reached behind her to grab a dark gray pencil to start sketching the contours.

She had just raised her pencil when footsteps approached the living room. John. Why wasn't he out in the field? She gazed towards the door where her husband had stopped. He looked pale, standing there in his blue trousers and shirt, his brown hair and beard neatly in order as usual.

She smiled. "Already back from the fie–"

"What are you doing?" His eyebrows were squeezed so tightly together that a crease had formed between them. He turned his brimmed straw-hat between his hands.

Martha's heart beat faster. John never spoke like that. "What does it look like I'm doing? Preparing a chicken soup?"

"It looks like you're drawing, that's what." He stepped closer, still fidgeting with his hat and frowning.

"Not yet, but I was about to start." The words came out hoarse. She cleared her throat.

Why was John so annoyed? Martha raised the pencil to her lips, about to bite, but stopped the movement at the last moment. Instead she pointed the pencil towards the window. "I'm going to draw that window."

"Drawing a window…" He snorted. "Don't you have more important things to do?" He crossed his arms over his chest, leaned back against the wall and wrinkled his forehead even more.

"This is important. To me. And besides…" She shrugged, "the children are all at school, so I have finally some time to spend for myself."

I've waited years for that to happen.

Of course she enjoyed being around her kids, but this was different. She measured the height of the window with her pencil, squeezing one eye shut. "It relaxes me. And

I love to create."

As she drew the first lines on the paper, John walked over to her and looked over her shoulder. "I always assumed it was just a whim when you started drawing. I thought you maybe feel alone when the children are in school, but that you would get used to it."

"A whim?" She clenched her teeth together so hard that it hurt. How could he know so little about her after all these years? Sure, they hadn't married out of love, but still…

Her hand was shaking slightly. With an effort she steadied it, then sketched the curtains and stood back to check the result. She nodded. Yes, this was going to be good. "Besides, I don't feel alone. I enjoy this."

Martha took a blue pencil and outlined the clouds, visible through the window. She didn't look at John as she continued.

"Ever since I was a little girl, I enjoyed drawing and painting. Of course, when we got married I didn't have time, and then there were the children… But now. Now I have the time to enjoy myself for an hour or so daily."

She turned towards him. "Surely, this isn't too much to ask for, is it?" She cocked an eyebrow.

When he didn't answer, she approached him and continued, "Don't I keep the house in order? And your clothes... Aren't they clean and ironed all the time? And aren't the children well-behaved?" She poked a finger in his stomach. "And what about food? Don't I cook and have the meals ready on time? I even help you with the animals, don't I?"

John looked at her as if she was a stranger. "What are you going to do with all those pictures of chickens and flowers?"

She closed her mouth. Was this genuine interest?

"I don't know yet." She went back to the easel and sketched a second cloud.

"This isn't Amish." His voice was shaking.

One of the clouds received a zig-zag line instead of the round shape she had intended. Not Amish? "What? What do you mean?"

"Drawing. Making art. That's not the Amish way."

Martha's jaw dropped. Was this against the Ordnung? Her mother had never forbidden her to draw. She hadn't encouraged her either, but Martha had stopped of her own free will. Never once had she questioned if drawing was frowned upon.

Surely this couldn't be wrong, could it? Her heart pounded so hart she was afraid of going deaf.

Then she shook her head. No. It couldn't be wrong. She was only drawing landscapes, lifeless things, animals or people at a distance. Faceless people.

She lifted her chin, meeting John's gaze. "If Gott didn't want me to draw, I'm sure He wouldn't have given me the talent."

To continue reading, click https://www.amazon.com/dp/B01E289PZ6 to buy.

Newsletter Sign-Up

Do you want to be the first to hear about new books, giveaways, offers, and more?

Then sign-up for my newsletter by clicking here or by going directly to my site at https://RachelYoderMay.com

Also by Rachel Yoder-May

Courting the Amish Widow

Naomi's Destiny

The Amish Hostage

Lost in Holmes County

Martha's Dilemma

Mary's Christmas Dream

The Amish Scribe

Collections

Amish Romance: Three Books in One (part 1)

Amish Romance: Three Books in One (part 2)

About the Author

Rachel Yoder-May lives with her family, her cat and dog, in a quiet neighborhood in a small rural town. She loves cooking and baking, walking her dog, and—most of all—reading and writing stories.

You can follow her on her blog at https://RachelYoderMay.com or on her Facebook page at https://www.facebook.com/rachelyodermay

She loves to meet readers, so please come by and say "hi" :)

Word List

Aenti = aunt

Ausbund = Amish hymnal

Boppli = baby

Bruder = brother

Datt = dad

Dawty haus = grandparent's house

Dokder = doctor

Dummheiten = foolish things, stupidities

Englisher(s) = non-Amish person(s)

Gesicht = face

Gmay = community

Gott = god

Guder mariye = good morning

Kapp = thin, white head cap

Kochoffe = Cook stove

Meedel = girl

Mem = mom

Mudder = mother

Neh = no

Onkel = uncle

Ordnung = the unwritten rules the Amish live by, differs from group to group

Rumspringa = period of freedom for an Amish youngster, before he/she decides to join or leave the Amish

Vadder = father

Vorsinger = the man who leads the song in a church service (pronounced with an F, as in Forsinger)

Wasser = water

Yah = yes (should probably be spelled 'jah', but the English pronunciation of J is different than the German/Pennsylvania Dutch way of pronouncing it)

LOST IN HOLMES COUNTY

Copyright © 2020 Rachel Yoder-May

All rights reserved.

This is a work of fiction. All characters and events portrayed in this book are fictional, and any resemblance to real people or incidents is purely coincidental.

You may not reproduce this book or parts of it in any form without written permission.